THE WIND IN THE WILLOWS

by KENNETH GRAHAME

#1 The Riverbank

Adapted by Laura Driscoll

Illustrated by Ann Iosa

Sterling Publishing Co., Inc.
New York

E
GRA

visit us at www.abdopublishing.com

Reinforced library bound edition published in 2008 by Spotlight, a division of the ABDO Publishing Group, 8000 West 78th Street, Edina, Minnesota 55439. Published by agreement with Sterling Publishing Co., Inc.

Originally published and © 2003 by Barnes and Noble, Inc.
Illustrations © 2003 by Ann Iosa
Cover illustration by Ann Iosa

Library of Congress Cataloging-in-Publication Data
This title was previously cataloged with the following information:

Driscoll, Laura.
  The wind in the willows. #1, The riverbank / by Kenneth Grahame ; adapted by Laura Driscoll ; illustrated by Ann Iosa.
    p. cm. -- (Easy reader classics)
    Summary: A brief, simplified retelling of the episode in "The Wind in the Willows" during which Mole meets Rat, who takes him for a row down the river for a picnic and introduces him to many other animals there.
    [1. Animals--Fiction. 2. River life--Fiction.] I. Iosa, Ann, ill. II. Grahame, Kenneth, 1859-1932. III. Title.
PZ7.D79 Wio 2006
[E]--dc22   2005026587

ISBN 978-1-59961-340-6 (reinforced library bound edition)

Contents

Spring!

Mole was tired of cleaning.
He had swept his house.
He had dusted his house.
He had cleaned
all morning long.
How he wanted to be out
in the fresh spring air!

So Mole ran outside.

He felt the warm sun.

He felt the soft breeze.

"This is great!" said Mole.

"This is better than cleaning!"

Mole ran and jumped.

He ran across meadows.

He ran past bushes.

He ran and ran and ran.

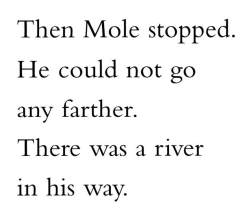

Then Mole stopped.
He could not go
any farther.
There was a river
in his way.

A river!
Mole had never seen
a river before.

Mole sat down
to look at the river.
On the other side,
he saw a hole
in the riverbank.
What was that?
Inside the hole
was a tiny light!

The light twinkled.
Then it winked
right at Mole!
It was an eye.

It was the Water Rat's eye!

The Water Rat

The Water Rat came
out of his house.
"Hello, Mole!"
called the Water Rat.
"Hello, Rat!" called Mole.

Rat got into his boat.

He rowed over to Mole.

He helped Mole get in.

What a day Mole was having!

"I've never been

in a boat before,"

Mole told Rat.

"What?" cried Rat.

Rat could not imagine

life without boats!

"How about we take a trip
down the river today?"
Rat said.
Mole loved the idea.
"Let's go!" said Mole.

A Picnic

Rat rowed home
and packed a picnic lunch.
Then he and Mole set off.
As Rat rowed,
he told Mole about
the river—
about the smells,
the seasons, and the food.
"It's my world
and I don't want
any other," said Rat.

Mole agreed that
it sounded great.
"But isn't it lonely?"
asked Mole.
"Just you and
the river,
and no one else?"

Very soon,
Mole would answer that
for himself.

Down the river,

Rat landed the boat.

Mole spread out their picnic.

They were eating

when Otter swam by.

He stopped to chat

with Rat and Mole.

Otter *loved* to chat.

Then they saw shy Badger
in the bushes.
But he rushed away
when he saw them all.
"Badger does not like
get-togethers,"
Rat told Mole.

Then Toad sailed by.
He was in his
brand-new boat.
He was wearing
brand-new clothes.
Toad liked new things.
Rat waved to Toad.

How wrong Mole
had been!
The river was not
lonely at all.

Home Again

Soon all the food
was eaten.
The sun was sinking low.
Mole packed up
the picnic basket.
He and Rat
got back into the boat.

As Rat rowed home,
Mole got to thinking—
rowing looked like fun!
He was sure
he could do it.

"Ratty," Mole said.

"Please, I want to row now."

He jumped up.

He took the oars

from Rat.

Mole tried to row,
but he missed the water.
He fell backward and . . .

. . . *splash!*

The boat tipped over.

Rat laughed.

He was right at home

in the water, but

Mole was not.

He could not swim!

Rat helped Mole to shore.
Then Rat dived for
the boat and the basket.
Soon Mole and Rat were
on their way again.
Mole felt terrible.
"I am very sorry,"
Mole said.

Rat was not angry at all.
In fact,
he invited Mole
to stay at his house
for a while.
"I'll teach you to row,
and to swim,
and all about river life!"
said Rat.

Mole was so happy.
He did not know
how to thank Rat.

But Mole
did know one thing.
He had two great
new friends—
Rat and the river.